D1146386

This book belongs to:

Keith A. Macpherson

from John & Ewan

Christmas 88

Postman Pat

Plays for Greendale

Story by **John Cunliffe**

Pictures by **Joan Hickson**

From the original Television designs by **Ivor Wood**

André Deutsch/Hippo Books

Published simultaneously in hardback by André
Deutsch Limited, 105-106 Great Russell Street, London
WC1B 3LJ and in paperback by Hippo Books, Scholastic
Publications Limited, 10 Earlham Street, London WC2H 9RX
in 1986
Reprinted 1987
Reprinted 1988

ISBN 0 233 97991 3 (hardback)
ISBN 0 590 70590 3 (paperback)

Made and printed in Belgium by Proost
Typeset in Souvenir by Keyline Graphics

Just by Greendale church, there is a
nice flat field. In winter Alf Thompson's
sheep nibble its grass. In summer it is
the Greendale cricket pitch. Alf takes
his sheep up on the hills; Miss Hubbard
comes with the mower to cut the grass
and Peter Fogg comes on his tractor,
with the big roller, to roll it flat.

All summer the games go on. On
Saturdays and Sundays the people of
Greendale come to watch, and have a
chat under the shady trees.

One summer, Greendale began to win.
They beat Natland, Kendal and
Levens, one after the other.

Ted said, "If we go on like this, we'll be
county champions."

Greendale went on winning.

Pat said, "We'd better go into training
for the big match. You never know; Ted
might be right."

So, every evening after tea, they practised hard. Pat practised batting in the field behind the barn.

Miss Hubbard bowled, and the twins
fielded. When the ball went into the
long grass, Jess could sniff it out.

Ted and Peter practised in the field by
the lake, throwing catches to each
other. Once, the ball went in the water.

Dorothy Thompson waded out in Alf's
big wellingtons, and fished it out.

The Reverend Timms practised
bowling on the vicarage lawn, and
broke a window.

Ted came the next day to mend it.

"It's no trouble," he said. "We've got to win, now."

At last, the big moment came. If Greendale could beat Pencaster, they would be top of the county.

Miss Hubbard cut the grass; then she made some rhubarb wine.

Mrs. Pottage, Dorothy Thompson and
Granny Dryden knitted new sweaters
for the team.

The Reverend Timms wrote a story about the team for the Pencaster Gazette.

Alf and Dorothy Thompson cleaned the
pads.

Dr. Gilbertson oiled the bats with her
best linseed oil.

Sam brought a new ball from
Pencaster.

Katy and Tom cleaned the gloves.

Mrs. Goggins made the posters, and the signs for the car park.

The day of the match came. Greendale was full of cars, and coaches and people. Everything was ready. The sun was shining.

Pencaster went in to bat first.

Pat was bowling.

"Here's a special delivery," he said. He
sent down a fast ball.
"Out!"

"And this ball will come First Class."

"Out!"

Two out in the first ten minutes. Not bad!
Pencaster batted well, but in the end
they were all out, for 250 runs.

It was Greendale's turn to bat.

Ted and Sam were first men in. Ted hit

a boundary, into the vicarage garden.

There was a sound of glass breaking.

"Oh, dear," said Pat. "There's another

job for Ted."

It was a good game.

Pat and Alf were the last men in to bat.

They needed fifty-one runs to win. Alf

hit two sixes. Now Pat was at the

wicket. They only needed thirty-nine

runs!

"Pat will do it, you'll see," said Granny
Dryden. Her knitting needles were
going at top speed.
Miss Hubbard began to open the
rhubarb wine.

Mick Waters was Pencaster's demon
bowler. He sent a spinner at Pat. Pat
hit it hard. Away it went, over the trees.
It splashed down in Alf's pond. Six.
Another ball. It was one of Mick's best.
Pat hit it into the churchyard.

Where was the ball? The fielders could not find it. (Peter Fogg found it months later. It was in a pile of manure.)

A new ball had to be brought out.

"Hooray!" Pat shouted. "Six for a lost ball."

"We're winning! Keep going!" Miss Hubbard shouted back.

They did keep going. Pat scored another fifteen runs. Alf scored twelve.

They had won!

They were the county champions!

"Hurrah! Hurrah!"

How the Greendale people cheered.

And how good Miss Hubbard's rhubarb
wine tasted!
She gave some to the Pencaster team,
to thank them for playing such a good
game.
"They've been good sports," said Mrs.
Goggins. Everyone agreed.

There was a lot of handshaking, and
smiling and hugging.
The Mayor of Pencaster gave the
Greendale team a big silver cup.
The Reverend Timms made a speech.
The Mayor made a speech.

They all had tea and cakes and paste
sandwiches, then it was time to go
home.

"Now that *was* a day to remember," said Pat, as he gave the cup a polish. "I wonder if we'll ever win it again?"